KT-447-856

Lin

Danny

Sam

"Nothing," said Lin. "Talent shows
are boring."

"No they're not!" said Britney. "You don't
have any talent. That's why you think
they are boring."

"We have hidden talent!" said Danny.

"Yeah!" said Clogger. "Well hidden!"

"Wow!" said Danny.

Lin looked puzzled. "Were his fingers supposed to come off?"

"Did you see where they went?" wailed Sam. "Help me get them back!"

"We're useless," said Lin. "Britney was right — we don't have any talent!"

"Don't be too sure about that," said Danny. "Let's team up! We could do a hot magic show..."

"It's us next. What happens if they don't like us?" asked Lin.

Danny grinned. "Don't worry. We'll knock them dead!"

Now I will turn my ordinary assistant into a wolf!

Hocus Pocus!

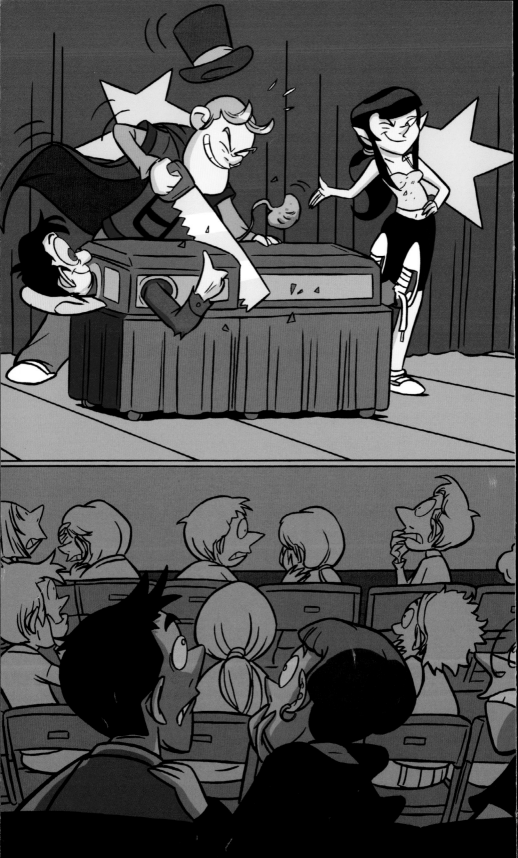

And to prove this is not a trick...

28